Acknowledgment
The publishers would like to thank John Dillow
for the cover illustration.

Ladybird books are widely available, but in case of
difficulty may be ordered by post or telephone from:

Ladybird Books – Cash Sales Department
Littlegate Road Paignton Devon TQ3 3BE
Telephone 01803 554761

Published by Ladybird Books Ltd Loughborough Leicestershire UK
Ladybird Books Inc Auburn Maine 04210 USA

© Illustrations GAYNOR CHAPMAN 1992
© LADYBIRD BOOKS LTD 1992 This edition 1994

About
wheels

by JACQUELINE HARDING
illustrated by GAYNOR CHAPMAN

In the morning the dustcart came to take the rubbish.

dustcart

The lady missed the bus.
What will she do?

bus

This truck had to stop at the side of the road!

truck

The big car towing
the caravan drove
round the truck.

caravan **car**

A horse trotted down
the road.
The motorbike went
past carefully.

motorbike

The tractor went slowly
along the road.

tractor

That car was
going too fast!

car

Beep! Beep!
The taxi was in a
hurry but there was
too much traffic.

taxi

A pickup truck broke down in the middle of the road.

pickup truck

A man helped to push the truck to the side of the road so that the traffic could get through.

traffic

A man in a
breakdown truck
came to look.

breakdown truck

So much traffic moving slowly ...except

the boy on his bike!